5-MINUTE LITTLE CRITTER® STORIES

BY MERCER MAYER

HARPER FESTIVAL
An Imprint of HarperCollinsPublishers

HarperFestival is an imprint of HarperCollins Publishers.

Little Critter: 5-Minute Little Critter Stories
Copyright © 2017 by Mercer Mayer.

ISBN 978-0-06-265525-7

Typography by Lori S. Malkin
17 18 19 20 21 SCP 10 9 8 7 6 5 4 3 2
❖
First Edition
A Big Tuna Trading Company LLC / J.R. Sansevere Book.
www.littlecritter.com

CONTENTS

THIS IS MY TOWN

Welcome to Critterville. This is my town. This is where I live with my family and neighbors. It's the only place I've ever lived, and I think it is the nicest place in the world. Today I am going to take you on a tour of all the places I like to go.

This is our post office. It is a very busy place. I come here to mail letters. I'm always careful to put a stamp on the envelope. Then I reach up high to drop my letter in the mailbox.

The postal workers collect the letters and sort them so they will go to the right places. Then they load the letters onto a mail truck, and away they go! A postal worker will deliver each letter to the right mailbox, come rain or shine.

This is our fire station.
The fire truck lives here.
Ooo! Eee! Ooo! go the sirens.
I cover my ears because the
sirens are very loud.

The firefighters are always ready to hop in the truck
when they are called. They wear long coats and helmets
to protect them when they fight a fire.

When there is a fire, the firefighters arrive on the fire truck. They use their ladders and hoses to put the fire out. The firefighters make sure everyone is safe. They teach everyone about fire safety before they leave.

This is our police
station. Police officers work here.
They wear blue uniforms with matching hats.
Police officers drive a special car. It has sirens
just like the fire trucks that tell people when there
is an emergency. It has a speaker, too. The police officers use
it to make announcements.

Some police officers are called detectives. They
look for clues and ask questions and solve mysteries.
I like to pretend I am a detective.
Police officers work together to keep our town safe.

This is our diner.
Sometimes I come here for
lunch with Mom and Dad
and Little Sister. I get a hot
dog and a milkshake. I put
the mustard on my hot dog
all by myself.

We have a movie theater
in our town, too. Sometimes
I get to go to the movies
with my friends.

I like to get popcorn at the
movies. I am always extra careful
not to drop it on the floor.

This is our town hall.
It's where all the important
business about our town
takes place.

Our mayor works here.
She runs the whole town
of Critterville. She is very
friendly.

Sometimes we have parades in our town. The streets are full of people and music and decorations. The mayor rides at the front of the parade in her car. She waves to everyone as she goes by. When she waves at me, I feel proud.

This is our library. I come here to find books to read. I use my library card to borrow books from the library to take home. Sometimes I take so many I can barely carry them all.

The library holds story hour every day. The librarian reads to us. He does different voices for each of the characters. We sit on the floor and listen.

This is our school. My friends and I are in Miss Kitty's class. She greets us at the door before school begins. She teaches us something new every day. School is fun!

There are lots of classrooms in my school.
Each classroom is for a different class.
I like my classroom with my friends the best.

This is our park.
Everyone comes here to go
for walks and play outside
and to find a quiet place to
sit. My friends and I play
football and baseball and
soccer here.

This is our bakery. It has
the best cupcakes. They are
a special treat.

This is our store.
You can buy almost
anything here. I save
my money to buy
gumballs for five
cents each.

Big Sale

5¢

So many great things happen in our town. You can read about them in the newspaper. It's called the *Critterville Scoop*. A lot of reporters work here because Critterville is such a busy place.

I was in the newspaper last week. My class planted trees for our town to enjoy. I like helping my town.

This is my town. It is full
of exciting places to go and fun
things to do.

But do you know what makes
Critterville the nicest place in the
whole world? It's the people who
live here. Everyone works together
to make our town great.

JUST BIG ENOUGH

Every morning on my way to school, I sit in the same seat on the school bus. I like my seat because it is between two of my friends. We talk and laugh all the way to school. It's the best!

But one morning a big kid took my seat.

I knew it was just a mistake. "Excuse me," I said. "You're sitting in my seat."

The big kid didn't move. He didn't even look at me. I guess he didn't hear me. I sat in another seat instead.

At recess, I saw the big kids playing football. I wanted to play football, too. But when I asked, they said I couldn't play because I was too small. That made me feel bad.

At lunch, the big kids got in line first and took all of the cupcakes. I told them that they had to share, but they only laughed at me. They told me the cupcakes were just for them. That didn't sound right to me. I was mad.

"I wish I were bigger," I said to my friends. "Then no one could sit in my seat on the bus or say I can't play football or take all of the cupcakes."

My friends agreed. They didn't get any cupcakes either. And I know they're good at football, too, because we play in the park together after school.

That night, I couldn't sleep. So I read
a comic book in bed. The story was about
a super-smart hero who built lots of
inventions to stop bad guys. And that's when
I got a great idea.

The next morning, I asked Mom and Dad
for some supplies. I needed wood, glue, and
tinfoil. Little Sister let me use some of her
art supplies, too.

"What are you making?" asked Little Sister.

"A growing machine," I said. "Just like the hero in my comic book." I carried everything out to the backyard. That would be my secret lab.

I worked on the growing machine all morning. When it was finished, I sprinkled glitter on it so it sparkled like the one in the comic book I had read.

I made a helmet and vest out of tinfoil. Then I put on my tinfoil suit and climbed into the growing machine. It was time to try my invention!

28

I sat in the growing machine all afternoon.

I read comic books. I took naps.

I even ate my lunch there.

When it became dark, Dad came out to my secret lab. "It's time to come inside," he said.

"Did I grow?" I asked. I sat up straight and puffed out my chest, trying to look as big as possible.

Dad looked at me very, very closely. He shook his head and smiled. "You look like the same Little Critter to me," he said.

"Maybe I should sleep in the growing machine," I said. Dad didn't think that was such a good idea.

The next day, I went to Grandma and Grandpa's farm.

"What's the matter, Little Critter?" asked Grandpa.

I told Grandpa all about the big kids at school and how I was trying to get big, too, so that I could do all the things the big kids did.

"I know just how you feel," said Grandpa.

"You do?" I asked. Grandpa was one of the biggest Critters I knew. How could he know what it's like to be little?

"Let me show you something," Grandpa said.

Grandpa took me out to the meadow.

"Look at those two horses," he said. "Which one do you think is the fastest?"

"The big one!" I said. That question was easy. "Am I right?" I asked.

"Let's see," he said. Grandpa let the big horse and the little horse loose. They started to run across the field. At first they were neck-and-neck, and then one pulled ahead. Do you know which one was the fastest? The little one.

I don't know how, but Grandpa knew just what to do to make me feel better.

The next day at school, I asked the big
kids again if I could play football. When they
said I was too small, I started to get mad.

"I challenge you to a relay race," I said.
"The big kids against the little kids."

The big kids laughed at first. Then they
saw that I was serious and they said okay.

The whole school came to watch the race. We lined up in the schoolyard, three little kids and three big kids.

I was nervous, but I ran as fast as I could. So did my friends.

And you know what?

35

The little kids won! We did
something better than the big kids
could, and that felt great. I didn't
feel so small anymore.

So, I guess sometimes being
small is just big enough.

JUST A SCHOOL PROJECT

We were having a science fair at our school. Miss Kitty said we were each supposed to do a special project. We would put them on display for all the parents and other students to see.

HELPING HANDS AND PAWS

WASH BOARDS — Gabby
CLOSE WINDOWS — Tiger
EMPTY TRASH — Molly
CLAP ERASERS — Bat Child
PENCIL SHARPENER — Gator
FEED HAMSTER — Little Critter

MISS KITTY

BIRD

MISTER NIBBLES

Tiger knew right away that he was going to do his project about rocks. "I'm going to show my collection of geodes," he said. "I'm going to look up information on all the different types of gems."

Gator decided to do his project about stars. "I can't wait to use my telescope," he said. "I can see stars in other galaxies from my backyard."

Gabby decided to do her project about horses. "I love taking care of my horse, Rey," she said. "I'll find out more about what keeps her happy and healthy."

Everyone had an idea except for me.

After school, I told Mom about my project. I told her I needed a really good idea.

"I know just the place to go," Mom said. She took me to the library. "We can ask the librarian for help," she said.

The librarian showed me the science section. I liked that section. There were lots and lots of books, and they gave me lots and lots of ideas. "Can I borrow more than one book?" I asked the librarian.

"Sure!" she said. I chose my favorite books and brought them all home.

First I made a rocket ship. I thought for my project I could show everyone that I could fly to the moon like an astronaut. But no matter how hard I tried, I didn't fly to the moon. I must have said "3, 2, 1, blastoff" a million times, but that didn't help. Dad said we had to cancel the mission for the night.

The next day,
I decided to dig for dinosaur
bones. I thought I could show everyone that I
could find fossils in my own backyard. I dug and dug,
but all I found was one of my dog's chewing bones.
She was willing to share it with me, but I
didn't think my teacher would think
it was very scientific.

After that, it was time for lunch. I sat on the step outside to eat. I took a big bite. Then I looked down, and right next to my sandwich I saw a caterpillar.

I had seen lots of caterpillars every spring, but I didn't know where they came from or where they went.

"Mom! Dad!" I shouted. "I know what I'm going to do my project about—caterpillars!"

They thought it was a great idea, and I had thought of it all by myself!

Dad helped me look up facts about caterpillars. I asked questions, and he typed them into the computer for me.

Did you know that a caterpillar starts its life as an egg? After it hatches, it eats leaves and flowers all day and all night long. I'm glad I'm not a caterpillar.

If caterpillars ate flowers, I thought the garden would be a good place to find some more. I looked in between the flowers and under rocks. Caterpillars sure were hard to find.

Eventually I found a bunch of caterpillars. They were different colors and sizes. They all had lots of legs and two small antennae on their heads.

I put the caterpillars in a special box so they could breathe but not escape. I gave them some leaves and some flowers so they would have something to eat. Once my project was over, I'd put the caterpillars back where I found them.

Dad and I went to the store to get some poster board, markers, and glue. "You sure need lots of stuff when you do a project," said Dad.

"I hope I didn't forget anything," I said.

When we got home,
I was so excited to
write my report on
the poster board that
I wrote it a little too big.
Dad had to go back to
the store and get more
poster board. I tried writing my

report in pencil first on the new poster board. It worked!

Then I drew some pictures of caterpillars and glued them
onto my poster, but the glue was a little too sticky.

When my report was finally done, it looked great! All the hard work was worth it. I knew so much about caterpillars!

Did you know that a caterpillar gets bigger by splitting its skin down the back and crawling out in a new skin?

A week later, it was time for the science fair. Everyone brought in a project. Someone even brought in a robot! I wanted to visit all the different tables, but I had to set up my project first.

I put up a sign in front of my table explaining my project. Dad helped me set up my poster board full of research. All I had to do was display my caterpillars.

Everyone gathered around my table.

I opened up my special caterpillar box, and do you know what?

A whole bunch of butterflies flew out!
That's because caterpillars turn into
butterflies when they grow up.
It was the best science project ever.

JUST ONE MORE PET

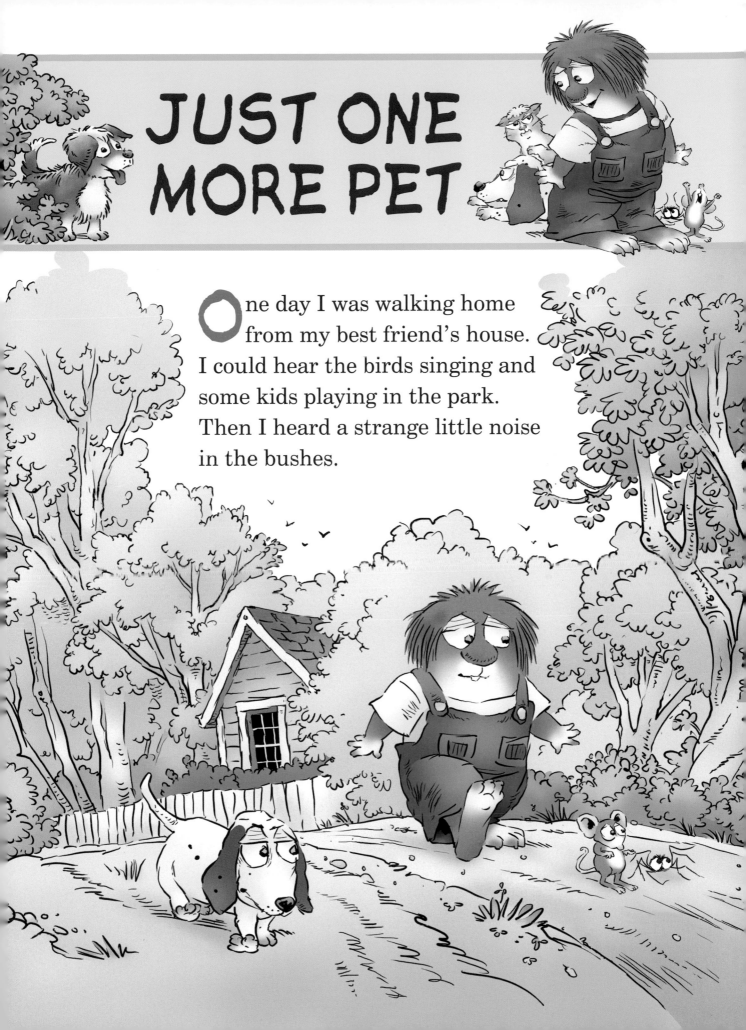

One day I was walking home from my best friend's house. I could hear the birds singing and some kids playing in the park. Then I heard a strange little noise in the bushes.

I pushed aside the bushes and couldn't
believe what I saw. It was a little doggy! He
was very friendly. He didn't have a collar.

"Are you lost, little doggy?" I asked.
He followed me home. What could I do?

"Mom!" I yelled when I got home. "Can we please keep him?" I asked.

When Mom saw who had come home with me, she was surprised.

"You have to take him back, Little Critter. We have too many pets," Mom said.

"He is lost and doesn't have a home," I pleaded.

Mom said we had to discuss it as a family, but we should make sure the little doggy was safe.

"He can stay in my room!" I said.

Mom let me tie him up in the backyard until Dad got home.

Our kitty did not like him. She puffed up her fur and hissed. I didn't think that was very nice.

Our dog did not like him, either. He barked and barked. The little doggy was scared. "That is not how you treat a guest," I told my pets.

I gave the little doggy a bath. He liked
that. He splashed in the water for a long
time and the bubbles went everywhere.

I took him to my room so he would be comfortable
for the night. That's when Little Sister saw him.

"I'm gonna tell," she said.

I had to give her a dollar just to keep her quiet.

Mom heard the doggy bark, and she made me
take him back outside.

The little doggy looked so sad. I decided to keep him company. I wanted my dollar back, but Little Sister wouldn't give it to me. The little doggy and I were both a little bummed about how things turned out.

When Dad came home, I showed the little doggy to him. He and Mom talked it over. "He can stay here until we find his owner," he said.

"What if we can't find his owner?" I asked. "Can I keep him?"

"Let's worry about that later," Mom said. But I was already worried about it.

We made a bed for the little doggy in our garage. I sang him a goodnight song and asked him to go to sleep, but the doggy barked and barked. He sounded lonely. He sounded sad.

I took my bath and got ready for bed, and the doggy still cried.

Dad read a bedtime story to me. We could hear the doggy whine the whole time. He was scared. I tried to sleep, but I could still hear the doggy.

It took a long time for me to fall asleep that night.

The next morning I went out to the garage to check on the doggy. He wasn't in his bed. He was gone! I looked all over the garage, but he wasn't there.

He must have escaped through a crack in the garage door.

I looked all around the yard and called and called. "Here, doggy! Here, doggy!" But the doggy didn't come.

I asked my dog and kitty, "Do you know where the doggy is?"

They were no help at all.

I ran next door to Mrs. Rhino's. "Mrs. Rhino, have you seen a little doggy in your yard?" I asked.

"No, I haven't. But somebody pulled all my clean sheets off the line," she said. She didn't look very happy.

I ran over to Mr. Bovine's house.

"Have you seen a little doggy in your yard?" I asked.

"No, I haven't. But somebody dug up my garden," he said. He was very upset.

I saw Mr. E. LePhant in his front yard.

"Mr. LePhant, have you seen a little doggy in your yard?" I asked.

"No, I haven't. But somebody chewed up my hose," he said. He was mad.

Mom and Dad and Little Sister all came to help me look. We asked all over the neighborhood, but no one had seen the doggy. We looked all over our yard, one more time, in case he was hiding. But we didn't find him.

When we got home again, I walked by the garage. I heard a bark and I ran inside. The doggy was back!

Only he was a she, and she was a mama. She had four little puppies.

I called everybody. "Oops! We have more doggies," I said. Little Sister was excited. Mom and Dad didn't say anything, but I bet they were excited, too.

Just then a car drove up.

Out of the car stepped a little girl and her mom. I had never seen them before. "Have you seen a little lost dog?" the girl asked.

I brought the girl to the garage. She was so happy when she saw the little doggy, but I was not.

"It is my dog!" she said. "And I even have puppies, too! Thank you for taking care of her!"

The little doggy barked. This time, she didn't sound sad or lonely. She sounded very excited.

The girl picked up a puppy and held it out to me. "Would you like to have a puppy after they get a little bigger?" she asked.

I asked Mom and Dad if I could.

After they talked it over, Mom and
Dad agreed. "Yes, just one more pet!"

GRANDMA, GRANDPA, AND ME

Tonight I am sleeping over at Grandma and Grandpa's house. They live on a big farm with lots of animals. It is my own special trip, just Grandma, Grandpa, and me.

I brought lots of fun toys for Grandma and Grandpa to play with. They have hardly any toys of their own. I wanted them to have the best time ever.

That night, I got to sleep in a big bed all by myself. I could stretch out and I took up the whole bed. But when it started to thunder and lightning outside I got a little scared.

But Grandma and Grandpa wanted me to sleep with them, because they don't like thunderstorms. I made them feel better. "It's just a storm," I said.

We woke up really early the next day, because Grandma and I had a big plan. We were going to make a pie to enter in a contest at the country fair. We had lots to do to get ready.

First I helped Grandpa milk the cows. I held the bucket steady, but the milk spilled a little. We didn't have to clean it up because it was outside. We asked the cow for a little extra milk.

Then I went to the henhouse to get some eggs. "Hello, hens!" I said.

"Cluck! Cluck!" went the hens. That's how hens say hello.

"How many eggs do we need, Grandma?" I asked.

"Just a couple," she said. "Do you know what kind of pie we're making?"

"No . . . ," I said. I was a little distracted. Gathering eggs from the hens was tricky.

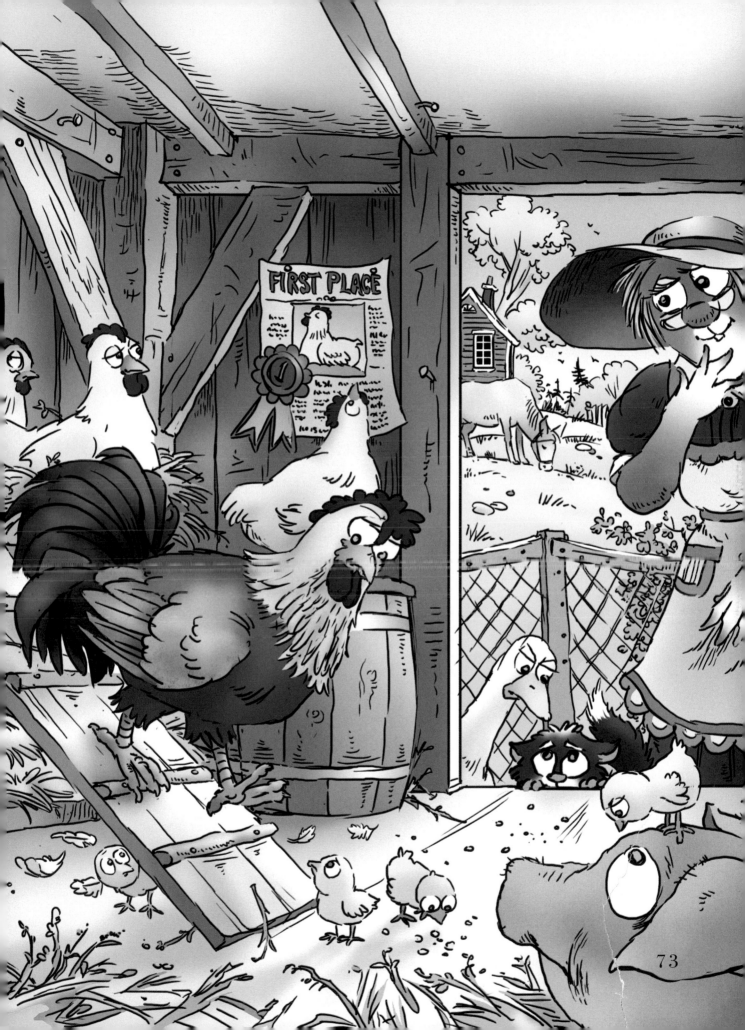

73

Next Grandma and I picked fresh berries for the pie.
We were going to make blueberry pie—my favorite! It was
hot out in the sun, but I was a good helper. I filled up my
whole basket—well, almost. I had to eat some to make sure
they were good enough to put in our pie.

Then it was time to make the pie. We washed up and got ready to bake!

We made the crust first. Grandma measured the ingredients to put in the bowl. Then I showed Grandma how to stir up all the ingredients with a big spoon. It's all in the elbow!

Then I rolled out the dough. It's kind of sticky, so you have to be really careful and use lots of flour on the rolling pin!

After that we poured sugar over the blueberries.
The sugar looked like an avalanche of snow, and
it made the berries taste even sweeter. In it went!
We mixed the blueberries and sugar and poured
the mixture into the crust. It looked so yummy
already! I couldn't wait to eat it. Then we put it in
the oven to bake.

Finally, I helped Grandma mix the eggs and milk together to make her special cream topping. It had to be just right.

"Please add lots of my secret ingredient," Grandma said.

"Where is it?" I asked.

Grandma pointed to her heart. She told me that lots of love makes a pie taste really good.

I could smell the pie baking, and I told Grandma that our pie already had lots of love in it.

Once the pie was done baking and cooling, we cleaned up. I made sure the frosting spoon was extra clean. That is a very important job.

At last, it was time to go to the country fair. Hooray! The fair was amazing. There were rides and games and people everywhere. Some people were entering vegetable contests and some were showing their livestock. We headed straight to the pie-judging booth to drop off the pie. I carried it the whole way all by myself, and sometimes I used only one hand.

When we got home, we all flew the kite I had
won for winning the ring toss. We had a really fun
day, Grandma, Grandpa, and me!

WE ARE MOVING

One night, Mom and Dad called Little Sister and me into the living room. "We have some exciting news," Mom and Dad said.

"Are we getting a new dog?" I asked right away. "A big fluffy one?"

"No . . . ," Mom said.

Little Sister thought hard. "Are we getting a new baby?" she asked. "Will *I* get to be a big sister now?"

"No," Dad said, smiling. Then they said together, "We are moving to a new house."

"That is horrible news!" I said. "You can't do this!"

Little Sister screamed and ran to her room. She stayed there until dinner.

At dinner Mom and Dad tried to cheer us up. "You will each get new rooms," Mom said.

"And you'll have new trees to climb and new memories to make," Dad said.

It didn't work.

"I like my room the way it is," Little Sister said.

I didn't want to make new memories. I liked the old ones just fine.

I went back to my room. The posters were
just where I wanted them. My bed was by the
window where I liked it. "Look at my room!
It's perfect!" I said. I will miss my room.

I went to the backyard and looked at my trees. I didn't like the thought of having to climb new ones. And where would we put the rope swing and the sandbox?

Then I thought of something huge. "Will I be able to take my tree house?"

I looked at my fence and realized I would have different neighbors. I didn't want to live next to strangers. They might even be monsters! I wondered if Dad had checked the new backyard for tentacles or slimy monster goo.

I wondered how far away my house would be. Maybe there wouldn't be any of my friends nearby. I wondered if I would have to take a bus, a train, and a boat to see them.

That would take forever. I wouldn't be able to see them every day. We couldn't meet after school to play anymore or on the weekends to play in the park.

"Oh, no!" I thought. What if I had to go to a new school? It could be full of bullies. I could have a really mean teacher. "I don't ever want to leave Miss Kitty's class!" I thought. "We have so much fun!"

Before long, Mom and Dad began cleaning out the house and garage. That was actually fun. I found some really neat stuff. Mom wouldn't let me keep any of it, though.

Mom said, "The Friendly Helping Critters are coming by to pick it all up. Now leave it alone."

I didn't want the Friendly Helping Critters to take our stuff. I wanted to keep it.

My friends came over to keep me company as Mom and Dad finished packing up our house.

"How far are you moving?" Tiger asked.

"I don't know," I said.

"Maybe we should play one last game of football," said Gator.

But we were too sad to play.

Finally, moving day arrived. A big truck came to our house. It had big tires and a really loud horn. There was a big space in the back for all of our boxes. "Will all of our stuff fit in that truck?" I asked.

"We'll see!" said Mom.

The movers began to move all of the furniture into the big truck. It was fun to watch them move the furniture out of the living room and my sister's room. Then they wanted to move my stuff. "No way," I said. I did not want any strangers touching my boxes.

"Let the movers do their job," Dad said.

"Okay," I said. "But my bear rides in the car with me."

Everything was packed in the truck. All of our boxes and furniture fit, but I was not impressed. "It's time to go," said Dad. I did not think it was time to go. I wanted to stay.

Dad had to carry me to the car. "It won't be so bad," he said. "You'll see." But I wasn't so sure.

Ve drove into the driveway of the new house. It was
"ect! It was even near my school.
!l my friends were waiting in front when we drove up.
lcome home!" they cheered. Tiger came running to our
"You've got some great climbing trees," he said.

"Yeah," said Gator. "And I can't wait to play football in the yard—it's huge!"

"What are we waiting for?" I asked. We picked teams and started the game. I made my first new memory at the house. It wasn't bad at all.

The house and yard were great. Sometimes
moving is not so bad after all.

JUST SAVING MY MONEY

One day I picked up my skateboard and the wheels fell off! "Oh, no!" I thought. I loved my skateboard. I rode it every day. But there was no way I could ride it without wheels.

I tried to put them back on but they wouldn't stay. When I stepped on the skateboard it creaked like it would snap. My skateboard was old and broken. I needed a new one. I told my dad.

"Wow, you really used that skateboard," he said. "You'll need money to buy a new one. Do you have any saved?"

"Yes!" I said. I ran up to my room and got my money jar. It was really heavy. "How about this?" I asked.

"Hmm," said Dad looking at all of the pennies and nickels. "A skateboard will cost more than that. You'll need to save some more," Dad said.

I was disappointed, but I wasn't worried. "I'll do chores and earn lots and lots of money. I'll be able to buy the best skateboard there is," I said.

I got straight to work. I made a list of chores. I thought of so many things I could do to earn money. I would have a new skateboard in no time!

First, I fed the dog, but the bag was too big. "Mom!" I yelled. She helped me clean up all the extra dog food. "Maybe you should try the next chore on your list," she said.

Next I tried to empty the dishwasher, but the dishes were heavy. I dropped some on the floor and they broke. "How about trying a chore that isn't in the kitchen," Mom said. I thought that was a good idea.

I cleaned my room. That chore was easy! I had everything put away really fast.

Finally, Mom paid me some money. I was on my way to getting a new skateboard.

COOL and FRESH
LEMONADE 25¢
BUY NOW

Next I sold lemonade in our front yard. It was a hot day, and everyone wanted a cool drink. For each cup I poured, someone put twenty-five cents in my jar. It was great! I got to have a little lemonade, too.

Soon I had so many dollars and coins they wouldn't
fit in the jar. I was proud.

I showed Dad. "You need a savings account," he said.
That sounded important and grown-up. "Okay," I said.

Dad took me to the bank. There were lots of people there to help. I wasn't sure I wanted to leave my money with all of these strangers, but Dad told me this is where grown-up critters put their money.

Dad told the manager that we had very important business. "We would like to open a savings account," he said.

"Oh, that is very important business," said the manager. "Right this way."

We followed the manager into an office. I held onto my money jar very tightly.

Dad wrote on some bank papers. Then, I wrote my name.

"Alright," said the manager. "All of your paperwork is in order. There is just one more thing to do—make a deposit!" Then the manager took my money jar. I was upset.

"Don't worry. You'll like this part," Dad said.

The manager gave it to the teller. "Mr. Critter would like to make a deposit into his savings account," he said.

"Very good!" said the teller. She poured my money into a machine.

It counted all the coins and bills. "You must have worked very hard to save up all this money," the teller said. I told her about all the chores I'd done!

The machine sorted my coins into rolls. Then the teller put the rolls of money into a vault. "I don't have a vault at home," I said.

Then I got a book that told me how much money I had. "Every time you put money into your savings account, we'll write it in this book. That way you'll always know how much you have," said the manager. "And you can come back and take your money out whenever you want."

"Like when I want to buy a skateboard?" I asked.

"Exactly," said the manager. "See you soon!"

I liked having a savings account. It was very official. "Hey, Dad," I asked as we drove home. "Can I get a skateboard yet?"

Dad said, "Not yet. You have to save more money."

Every day I did chores to earn more money. I worked in the garden.

I cleaned up the yard. I took out the trash.

It was a lot of work and a lot of waiting. But the more chores I did, the easier they got.

Finally I had saved enough money for a new skateboard.

"Congratulations!" said Mom. "You're going to love your new skateboard even more than the last one."

"Why?" I asked.

"Because you earned it!" she said, and gave me a big hug.

Dad helped me take the money I needed out of the bank. Then we went to the toy store. But when I got there, I realized I didn't want a skateboard anymore. I wanted something else instead—a Robot Dinosaur!

Dad let me carry my Robot Dinosaur to the car.
"Dad," I said. "I am so glad I saved my money!"
Mom was right. It felt great to have earned my own toy.

THE LOST DINOSAUR BONE

Our class went on a field trip to the Museum of Natural History. I couldn't wait to see the dinosaurs. I had already read all the books on them in the library, but I had never seen a dinosaur bone.

"Come along, class," said Miss Kitty.

"When I grow up, I'm going to be a dinosaur hunter," I told her.

"Then this trip is perfect for you," said Miss Kitty. "You're going to learn a lot!"

But when we got inside the museum, we got
some bad news. "I'm afraid the dinosaur exhibit
is closed until further notice," said a museum
worker. "But you can see the butterfly exhibit
instead. It's much livelier."

The butterfly exhibit was fun. We got to run around and touch everything. A butterfly even landed on my finger! It was cool, but I really wished we could see the dinosaurs.

Next we went to the Rain Forest exhibit. There were lots of trees with monkeys in them.

"Oooh! Oooh!" I said to the monkeys. They didn't say anything back, so I tried saying "Eee! Eee!" and "Uh! Uh! Uh!"

A guard came running over to see the monkeys, too, so I asked him about the dinosaurs. I found out that the exhibit was closed because a Triceratops bone was missing!

"Bones don't just walk away," I thought. The missing bone had to be around here somewhere.

118

"Stay together, class," said Miss Kitty. It was time to go to the next exhibit, the Hall of Gems and Minerals. We got to wear miner hats with lights on them while we looked at the stones. Tiger went looking for diamonds. He loves rocks.

I was busy looking for the missing dinosaur bone. No luck in there!

DIAMONDS IN ROCKS

After that, we went to the planetarium, where the ceiling turned into a sky filled with stars. "We are part of a vast expanding universe," said the planetarium host. "In our solar system alone, there are planets, moons, comets, asteroids, and of course, the Sun."

He told us that the planet Mars is covered with dust and that the planet Saturn has rings around it. I listened very carefully, but I kept my eye out for the missing dinosaur bone. I didn't see it.

120

On our way to see a meteorite, I asked Miss Kitty if I could get a drink of water. I promised I wouldn't wander off.

When I found the fountain, I also found something else— the dinosaur exhibit! It had a big sign saying EXHIBIT CLOSED. Past the sign, I saw something moving in the dark.

I went closer and saw a Tyrannosaurus rex. It was heading right for me!

I screamed and ran away as fast as I could . . .

. . . and found myself face-to-face with a Velociraptor. "Yipes!" I said. It had its mouth open wide so I could see all of its sharp, pointy teeth.

Finally a guard found me. Boy, was I glad to see him! "The exhibit is closed because of a missing dinosaur bone," he explained.

"I know," I said. "I've been looking for it everywhere. This museum is huge!"

On my way out of the dinosaur exhibit, I took a wrong turn. That's when I saw something long and white sticking out from under the Ankylosaurus skeleton.

"Could it be?" I thought. I took a closer look. It definitely didn't belong with the Anklylosaurus skeleton. It was the missing Triceratops bone!

"Guard!" I yelled, but I couldn't wait for him to find me again.

I ran back to the guard. I tried to explain as fast as I could. "I found it! I found it! I found the missing dinosaur bone. Now you can reopen the exhibit," I said.

He didn't believe me at first . . .

. . . but when I showed the bone to him, he gave me a big smile. "Why don't you go get your teacher," he said.

I followed the signs to the meteorite exhibit and found Miss Kitty and my class. The guard explained what happened and invited our whole class to the special place where the scientists who study dinosaur bones work. I was so excited.

"Thank you for solving the mystery of the missing Triceratops bone," the scientists told me.

"My pleasure!" I said.

GNATHUS
RY TINY
OSAUR

DIRT DAWG

The scientists took us on a tour of the dinosaur exhibit. They showed us the Stegosaurus skeleton they had found buried in a mountain. They answered all of my questions, too.

"I'm going to be a dinosaur hunter when I grow up!" I said.

"You already are," answered the scientists.

You know what I'm going to do tomorrow?
Dig for dinosaur bones in my backyard!

JUST A LITTLE LOVE

This morning the phone rang. It was Grandpa calling with bad news. He said Grandma wasn't feeling very well.

"I don't want Grandma to feel bad," I said.

"Me neither," Little Sister said.

"Well, there's something we can do," Dad said.

Mom finished his thought. "Give her a little love!"

We called Grandpa back and told him we were coming for a visit. He said Grandma would love that, so we got to work.

I drew a get-well card just for Grandma. Little Sister
helped. We used all the happy colors so the card would
be bright and cheerful, just like Grandma.

Mom made a special snack, egg salad. She put olives in it. I love olives, but I spilled them. Some of them rolled off the counter and onto the floor.

"Look, Mom," I said. "Blue loves olives, too!"

"I'm glad someone gets to enjoy them," Mom said.

"I know what will cheer up Grandma," Little Sister said. "Flowers!" She ran outside to pick a bouquet just for Grandma.

She liked gathering flowers until a bee stung her. She cried and cried. "It hurts!" she said. But after Mom gave her a little love, she felt better.

"It doesn't hurt that bad anymore," she said.

Next we picked apples for Grandma. We put them in a basket. Even though I was very careful, I missed a step on the ladder and fell.

I didn't cry much. "There, there," Dad said. "All you need is a little love." I felt better.

"I'll carry the apples to the
car," I said. I picked up the basket, but I didn't see Blue
walking right beside me. I accidentally stepped on her tail.
"Yelp!" Blue said.

I felt bad. I
didn't mean to
hurt her. "I'm
sorry," I said,
giving Blue a belly
rub. After a little
love, Blue felt
better.

After we got the apples in the car, we went to gather the rest of our surprises in the house. Little Sister wanted to bring her dolls to show Grandma.

Mom said, "Pick two to show Grandma, and leave the rest here."

Little Sister put away all but two dolls and came out of her room to give a report. "My other dolls are lonely," she said. "They need lots of love."

"I'm sure you can help them feel better," Mom said. "You have lots of love to give."

When Mom got to the kitchen, there was another surprise waiting for her. Not a good one, though. Kitty had found the egg salad and was sharing it with Blue! "Now we have no egg salad to bring to Grandma," Mom said. She was sad.

"That's okay, Mom," I said, giving her lots of love. "They are enjoying it!"

"Okay," Mom said. "We'd better get on the road, egg salad or not." Everyone got up to leave, but I stopped to say good-bye to my pets. They looked sad. I wanted them to have a little love before we left.

"We'll be back soon," I told them, and gave them both a hug.

We were almost to the car when
I spotted someone else who needed love. It was a
turtle in the middle of the road. "Dad!" I said. "Save the
turtle. Turtles need love, too."

Dad picked up the turtle and put him in the grass. I was
glad that he was safe. We waved good-bye and drove off to
give Grandma our love.

"I can't wait to hug Grandma," I said.

"Me neither," Little Sister agreed.

Soon a man on a motorcycle with flashing lights told Dad to pull over. He was a state trooper.

"Do you know how fast you were going?" he asked Dad.

The state trooper gave Dad a ticket, but not the kind for a ball game.

As the state trooper pulled away, Dad did not look too happy. We knew what to do. We gave Dad a little love so he would feel better. It worked! Dad drove nice and slow the rest of the way.

When we arrived at Grandpa and Grandma's house we got a good surprise. Grandma was not in bed. She was sitting on the porch with Grandpa. "Hi, kids!" she called out, waving to us.

"Grandma," I said. "I thought you weren't feeling well."
"I wasn't," she said. "When I heard you were coming, I felt much better! I just needed a little love."

I said, "Me, too, Grandma!"

GOING TO THE FIREHOUSE

Today my class went to the firehouse! I dressed like a fireman. "Time to fight a fire!" I thought.

CRITTERVILLE

FIRE HOUSE

When we arrived, we met Firefighter Joe and his dog, Sparky. They were very nice.

"I'll be showing you around the firehouse today," Firefighter Joe said.

"First, I'd like you to meet Sparky. Sparky is a fire dog. He works at the firehouse and rides with us in the fire truck."

Sparky liked me.

"This is where we keep our gear," Firefighter
Joe said. He showed us his boots, jacket, and
helmet. "They help keep firefighters safe when
they're working," he explained.

My firefighter outfit had boots and a jacket, too,
but I did not have a helmet like Firefighter Joe.

"Time to check the truck," Joe said. He drove the fire truck in front of the firehouse so he could check all the parts. The truck was big and red. It had a hose and ladder. It also had lights and a siren. "Those are so that people know we are coming and can get out of the way," Joe explained.

Joe let me help with the hose. He held onto the hose while another firefighter turned on the water. *Whoosh!* The water came out very fast and went far. The whole yard was soaked! "I think the hose is working fine," I said.

"I agree," Joe said.

"Now I'll check the ladder," Joe said. "During a fire, this helps us reach windows and roofs on tall buildings."

I did not help him with this part.

Joe climbed on top of the ladder while another firefighter worked the controls. The ladder went up, up, up in the sky. "Hello, down there!" Joe shouted to us. "I think the ladder is working."

"I agree!" I shouted back.

"Cover your ears while I check the siren," Joe said. He climbed inside the truck and turned on the siren. It went *Ooo! Eee! Ooo!* very loudly.

I covered my ears. "I think the siren is working," I shouted.

"What?" Joe shouted back. Then he turned off the siren.

"I think it's working," I repeated.

"I agree." Joe smiled.

After we checked the fire truck, we got to become fire safety experts. Joe told us that smoke goes up. And when smoke goes up, we must go down to the floor. "Like this?" I asked, crouching down low.

"Perfect," Joe said.

We practiced what to do if we were ever on fire. Stop, drop, and roll!

I stopped,

dropped,

and rolled.

"Good job," Joe said. I did it exactly right.

"Now that you are all fire safety experts," Joe said. "I have a surprise for you." We followed Joe out to the fire truck. I couldn't image how this day could get any better. Then Joe opened a compartment and pulled out helmets for everyone!

"Alright!" I said. I put on my helmet. "Do I look like a firefighter?" I asked Joe.

"Absolutely," Joe said. "And you will be a good firefighter one day, too."

"I agree," I said.

Just then the fire alarm went off. It rang *Ding! Ding! Ding!* like a bell. The firefighters slid down the pole, put on their gear, and jumped on the truck in seconds, just like Joe showed us.

As the fire truck pulled away, I waved good-bye to Firefighter Joe and Sparky. "Time to put out a fire," I thought.

Firefighter Joe is ready to go! Sparky is, too.

JUST A
EACHER'S PET

...ame to our school. We saw her

..."Stay here, class. I'll be

righ...

We... ...as we could, but we really
wante... s fun ... ...snuck a peek. "I'm Miss
Kitty," o... trimmed, Dad
to the new ... nails. "Step
know you w...
at home in o... ok good

Miss Kitty ...
new student sta... a jet pack.
to move toward t...
door. "Here they
come," I said. "Quick,
everyone sit back
down."

"Class," said Miss Kitty. "Say
hello to our new student, Bunella."

"Hi, Bunella," we all said together.

"Hi," Bunella said and gave Miss
Kitty an apple. Miss Kitty smiled
and said she loved apples.

162

"That's weird," I thought. No one else gave Miss Kitty apples.

Bunella made herself comfortable at the desk right in the front. That was weird, too! Nobody ever wanted to sit in the front desk. "Why would she want to sit there?" I wondered.

Soon we could tell that Bunella wasn't
like the rest of our class. She raised her hand
first. She passed out work sheets. She turned in her class
work first. I wasn't sure I liked having Bunella in my class.

When the bell rang, we all got up to go home, except
Bunella. She stayed to clean the blackboard.

"Thank you, Bunella," Miss Kitty said.
"She's going to miss the bus," I thought.

167

Outside, my classmates and I got on the bus and sat in our usual seats. But the bus didn't move.

"Is something wrong with the bus?" I asked.

"No," said the bus driver. "We are waiting for the new student. She was staying late to help the teacher."

"We know!" all the kids groaned.

Just then, Bunella came out of the school and climbed on the bus. "The bus doesn't wait for any other kids," I thought. Bunella must be the teacher's pet.

The next day we had a class trip. We went to the museum. It was supposed to be fun, but Bunella ruined everything! She was the teacher's helper for the day.

"Stand over there," she said. "Say 'here' when I call your name," she said. Bunella was taking attendance!

Bunella wouldn't let us enjoy any of the exhibits. She watched us like a hawk.

"Don't touch that," she said.

"Watch where you are going," she warned.

When it was time to go back to school, Bunella made us stand in a line. "I'm going to count you to make sure you're all here," she said. I rolled my eyes just a little. I couldn't help it.

Once we were back at school, we went to the auditorium
for a program. The teacher's pet still wouldn't leave us alone.
She said we were too noisy. Every time we spoke, she stood in
front of us and said, "Hush!" She was spoiling all of our fun!

I just wanted my class to be back to normal, like before
Bunella came. That wasn't bad, right? I remembered Miss
Kitty telling Bunella that she'd be right at home in our class.
I wish I could tell Miss Kitty how wrong she was. Bunella
was not fitting in at all.

Thankfully, we got out of school early that day. When the bell rang, we all cheered and ran out to the school yard. We had a ball game with the other grade.

"They always beat us," Tiger said.

"But at least while we are playing, the teacher's pet can't tell us what to do," I said. Maybe I spoke too soon.

We were just getting our lineup figured out when Miss Kitty came over to the team.

"Tiger will bat first," I said.

"And then me?" Gator asked.

"And then you," I said. "Just like always."

"Don't forget to invite your new classmate to play," Miss Kitty called out. Everyone groaned, but I felt bad. Bunella hadn't made any friends at school, and I hadn't tried to make Bunella feel at home at all.

"Come on, Bunella," I said. "There's room for you on our team."

Soon the bases were loaded, and it was Bunella's turn to bat. I closed my eyes. I knew she would ruin our chances of winning. I just couldn't watch.

Then Bunella surprised us all. The ball soared right over home plate and *crack!* Bunella hit a home run! "Go, Bunella, go!" we cheered as the ball flew over the fence. Bunella ran around the bases with a big smile on her face. "She is a lot more fun when she's playing with us," I thought.

We won the game by one run. "Hip-hip-hooray!"
we all chanted as we hoisted Bunella in the air.
Bunella looked right at home.

She may be the teacher's pet, but we all want
her on our team.

JUST CRITTERS WHO CARE

One afternoon, I was playing baseball at Tiger's house. Tiger pitched the ball right over the plate. I hit the ball hard, maybe a little too hard!

The ball flew way up high and landed in the next-door neighbor's yard. "Whoops!" I said. "I'll get it."

"I don't know if you should go over there,"
said Tiger. "That yard is spooky." Tiger's voice
shook a little. "I think a monster lives there,"
he said.

"A monster?" I thought. "I'm not afraid of
monsters! I'm brave."

"I'll run and get the ball very fast, before any monsters even know I'm there," I said to my friends. "Ready, set, go!" I said.

I started running. I ran very fast. "Almost there," I thought. "Just a few more—" But before I could reach the ball, I tripped and fell. All of my friends gasped.

"Look out, Little Critter!" they called.

When I looked up, I
saw a little old bunny. She
handed me our ball. I got to my feet.
"Thank you," I said. I am always polite.

"No trouble at all," she said. "Be careful so you don't
trip again."

"I will," I said. "Good-bye!" I ran back to my friends.

181

"Tiger! There's no monster there," I said. "A nice old bunny lives in that house."

"Then how come we never see her?" Tiger asked. "And why does her house look so . . . spooky?" I didn't know the answers to his questions. "I'll be back tomorrow," I said.

182

At home, I asked my dad why the old bunny's house looked so spooky.

"Mrs. Bunny is not feeling well," Dad said. "And she has no one to help her keep the yard clean."

That made me sad. I need lots of help every day. Mrs. Bunny must want someone to come help her. Then my sister and I get a great idea.

"We can help Mrs. Bunny! We are critters who care," I said.

"That's a great idea," Dad said. "We'll all help."

I called up my friends and explained our plan. "What a great idea. We'll help, too," they said.

"Great! Meet at my house tomorrow," I told them. I was excited to get started. "Mrs. Bunny will be so surprised," I thought.

"We need T-shirts!" I said. "That way, people will know they can come to us for help."

I made the picture for the T-shirts. Little Sister colored in the bright red heart. Then Dad had our picture printed on the T-shirts.

It was official. We were Critters Who Care!

The next day, my friends met at my house.
Their parents came, too. They brought tools and
supplies to do yard work and make repairs. We gave
everyone T-shirts. We looked great wearing our bright
red hearts.

"To Mrs. Bunny's house!" I called.
"Hooray!" they said.

When we got to the spooky yard, this time I wasn't scared. I walked straight up to the front door and knocked. Mrs. Bunny opened the door. "Hello," I said. "We are Critters Who Care! May we do some yard work for you?" I asked.

"Why, yes!" Mrs. Bunny said. "Thank you!"

Tiger got to work mowing the lawn.

trimmed the hedges.

Little Sister pulled weeds out of the ground.

ad trimmed the tall trees.

Ouch," said Little Sister. "These weeds hurt

ands."

"You can borrow my gloves!" I said. It wa[...]
to have everyone working together.

We didn't stop there! Once the trees were [...]
fixed the porch step. It just needed a few new [...]
right up!" Dad said cheerfully.

Tiger's dad fixed the shutter. "This will lo[...]
as new!" he said.

I used the leaf blower. It was powerful like [...]
"I can handle it, no problem!" I said.

Little Sister raked.

e working together, the yard was cleaned

like we did it," Dad said. But there was
o would be the judge of that—Mrs. Bunny.
out of the house, we all gathered around
at she'd say. "I'm not sure this yard
oked so good," she said. "I can't thank
h."

"Hooray!" we cheered.

Mrs. Bunny gave everyone juice and cookies. Of course, I helped carry the cookies. They were chocolate chip, yum!

Once we finished our snack, it was time to say good-bye. "But we are still Critters Who Care," I said. "What should we do next?"

Little Sister had a great idea. "We could get toys for kids who don't have any," she said.

"If anyone can do it, we can!" I said. "Let's get to work!"
Everyone agreed.